·DragonQuest·

ALLAN BAILLIE & WAYNE HARRIS

CANDLEWICK PRESS

HEY, YOU!

Yes, yes, you with the book!

Up, up, we have deeds to do!

Bold deeds,

deeds so daring that songs

will be sung for a thousand years.

Come on! You'll be a hero,

a great warrior, an epic knight.

Here, carry my lance,

my shield, my stew pot.

Our quest? Ah, yes.

But first we must pass many
perils out there. Awful perils,
dangers to set your teeth chattering,
to turn your hair white.

And after we have fought through
them all?

Then we must face the worst of
terrors — green ice gleaming in
the eye, claws flashing in the smoky
sun, fire curling from its mouth. . . .
Now, there's a grand quest!

Waiting for us is the last dragon.

But the dangers start now!
In these shifting sands
lie the bones of noble knights,
perished with their swords undrawn.

We must watch for the sting
of scuttling scorpions,
the hundred bites
of the banded wasps,
and we must always be ready
for the lightning strike
of the deadly desert snakes.

Can you see them?

We have crossed the desert.

Of course I knew we would.

I am too fast for any snake —

I am so fast even my own shadow

cannot catch me.

There was no need to be afraid.

But there are dark dangers in this tangled forest.

Here are spitting toads, poisonous webs, ghost owls, wolves, goblins.

And worse, three dark witches coil evil spells through the forest.

Listen. You can hear the howling of doomed dragon fighters,
trapped in the witchery of the trees.

But you see,

we have cleared the forest.

There was no need to be afraid.

I am as strong as ten elephants,

brave as a score of lions.

Be careful now,

of the whispering abyss.

Fanged werewolves

will leap out at you,

thorned demons

will nibble at you,

and if you fall,

a fright of vampire bats

will drink you dry before

you reach the bottom!

Shhh . . .
We must be quiet —
a double-headed troll
lurks in these hills.
And a double-headed troll
can never be defeated in battle.
It commands a flight of vultures,
an army of warrior gnomes,
a stampede of centaurs.

AWOOH! COWARDLY NAG!

All right, we don't need the horse.

Now, see, we're out of troll country — there was no need to be afraid.

A double-headed troll cannot be defeated —

but it can be outwitted.

If the double-headed troll had seen us, I would have asked to speak with its head head.

Then the heads would have fought about which of them is the head head.

You are very lucky to be around such a smart dragon fighter.

Glass Mountain.

Dragon country, at last.

No, no, don't worry about falling
rocks. Always look up at the sky.
If the dragon is flying and it sees us,
we are doomed.

There is nothing you can do
about a flying dragon.

Right, this is it.

The top of Glass Mountain.

No dragon can hide from me

in a cloud.

Pass me my lance and shield.

Prepare for a mighty battle!

Why? What do you mean, *why?*

You don't want me to fight it?

You just want to see a dragon,

to know it's there?

What's the good of that?

What's the good of a dragon fighter

who doesn't fight dragons?

Never heard of such a thing!

What! Nothing here? Can *you* see any dragons?

Look to the glittering ice, to the polished sea, the shifting sands, the forest. . . .

No? No dragon at all? No dragon left anywhere.

Nothing to do but go home.

BUT WHY ARE YOU GRINNING?

First U.S. edition 2013

Library of Congress Catalog Card Number 2012950624
ISBN 978-0-7636-6617-0

SCP 18 17 16 15 14 13
10 9 8 7 6 5 4 3 2 1

Printed in Humen, Dongguan, China

This book was typeset in Chaparral.
The illustrations were done in acrylic and digital media.

Candlewick Press
99 Dover Street
Somerville, Massachusetts 02144

visit us at www.candlewick.com

*This illustration was originally intended for the cover of DragonQuest,
but we decided not to use it because it didn't look like the dragon in the
book, and to use the dragon in the book would give the story away.*

· DRAGON QUEST ·

This has long been one of my favorite picture books, and now a whole new generation of readers can enjoy it.

I particularly love the interaction of Baillie's words with Harris's images, especially at the end of the story, when words and pictures tell different stories and the reader shares in the wonderful secret.

Many of Baillie's stories have been about boys learning to become men — and what better way than by joining a veteran dragon fighter on a dangerous quest to find and slay the last dragon. There are of course terrible obstacles to overcome: a desert inhabited by deadly snakes, scuttling scorpions, and banded wasps; a tangled forest haunted by "the witchery of the trees"; "a whispering abyss"; and hills patrolled by two-headed trolls. And finally there is the last dragon — and the boy's recognition that it is more heroic not to kill. The reader shares the boy's triumph on the final wordless page.

This is a book for reading and rereading. Baillie's words beg to be read aloud to hear them resonate. Harris's paintings are rich in detail, with new discoveries to be made on each viewing. *DragonQuest* is much loved by everyone who enjoys fantasy quests. For boys, it is also a delightful exploration of what it means to be a man.

Helen Sykes,
secondary English publisher, Cengage Learning Australia

FROM
ALLAN BAILLIE:

DragonQuest started with the marvelous words what if? And a mutter from an artist friend about working from a real dragon. That's all that was needed . . . and a flea.

In 1993, we had a Labrador-Alsatian cross, and I was looking for ticks and fleas on it while I was thinking about the dragon. I wanted a magnificent, mighty dragon, and then I saw a flea on the dog. Nothing happened then, but I guess the machinery of the mind was working. Another day I was thinking that I had a knight and boy hunting for a dragon — but *what if* this dragon was enormous? So big that they would climb the dragon, like fleas climbing a dog, without knowing it, and the reader wouldn't know, either?

I called the book *DragonSlayer,* and I sketched the dragon, just to show where the desert, forest, hills, and mountains would be. But when my artist friend decided that it wasn't the right project for him, I showed it to freelance editor Donna Rawlins. She wanted a rewrite and a better title, but she did show it to Wayne Harris, and he agreed to illustrate it.

After seven drafts, a new title — *The Last Dragon* — and two years, Wayne was showing us the final page of the book. Donna and I were nervous because the whole book hangs on that page. Then I saw it: "Yes! Yes! Great!" Nothing could stop us now.

But suddenly a new book called *The Last Dragon* hit the stores — not our book!

Quickly, we had to change the title of *The Last Dragon,* and somebody thought of *DragonQuest.* . . .

And now we have an American edition!